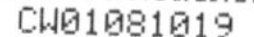

Mike Gould was born in the Somerset town of Midsomer Norton, between the city of Bath and the Mendip Hills. He grew up in the town when it was part of the Somerset Coalfields and spent most of his working life in the electrical industry.

The telling and writing of stories was requested by his three children when they were younger as the published stories of the day became exhausted. He continues with both story-writing and painting to this day.

To Lily
Best Wishes
from
Mike Gould

Trouble in Fairy Wood

Also by Mike Gould

Magic in Fairy Wood

Mike Gould

Trouble in Fairy Wood

Nightingale Books

NIGHTINGALE PAPERBACK

A CIP catalogue record for this title is
available from the British Library.

ISBN 978 1 912021 61 1

Nightingale Books is an imprint of
Pegasus Elliot MacKenzie Publishers Ltd.
www.pegasuspublishers.com

First Published in 2018

Nightingale Books
Sheraton House Castle Park
Cambridge England

Printed and Bound in Great Britain

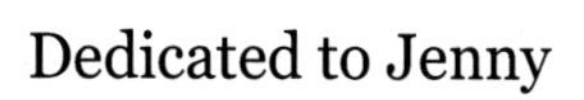

Dedicated to Jenny

Chapter 1

This is the Problem

Ben and Sue were having their breakfast of cornflakes and milk in the farmhouse kitchen. They were listening to their father, who was the farmer, talking to his farm manager.

The children were getting very worried because of what their father and his manager were talking about.

The manager was saying that to increase the crops they would have to remove several hedge banks and hedges around the fields to make the fields bigger, and easier to manage, including the hedge bank between eightacre field and the old wood.

The children knew the old wood was known by many people as Fairy Wood. They had some different and interesting adventures in Fairy Wood in the past, but they were not sure, as the adventures may have been a dream.

The discussions between their father and the manager went on for a long time until the children heard their father say, “We must now look to remove these hedge banks as soon as possible before we sow next year’s barley seed.”

The children looked at each other. They both knew what they had to do.

In the past both Sue and Ben were sure they had met some strange woodland creatures in Fairy Wood who had been very kind to them, and so they decided to go into the wood to try to find them again.

After breakfast they set off across eightacre field and into the wood.

It was a warm summer morning with little insects buzzing around in the air. Ben thought that some of the insects looked like tiny fairies just hovering in the sunlight.

The children wandered around the wood until they came across a large grassy bank, with a thick green hazel hedge growing on top of the bank.

The children had been searching for a long time and were getting very tired. They knew that what they were looking for was somewhere in this part of the wood, but neither of them could remember exactly where it was, or what it looked like. They both sat on the ground resting their backs against the hedge bank. The sun was warm on their faces, and they had to partly close their eyes against the sunshine.

A short time went by, when, the children saw some old leaves on the ground in front of them near their feet move very slightly. Ben tapped Sue on the arm and pointed to the place where the leaves were moving. Sue nodded in reply and they both looked very hard at the leaves.

Without any warning, the leaves sprang to life with the leaves and twigs flying in the air all around their feet; and there, looking at them with a big smile was a black mole wearing a large pair of spectacles. Neither of the children moved an inch, but just stared at the little animal in front of them.

Eventually Ben said, “Hello, are you Mr Mole?”

The mole did not reply, instead he raised his paw in the air, and pointed to a small brown door in the hedge bank.

In a flash the mole was gone. Sue said to Ben, “Did you see that mole?”

Ben nodded his head in agreement. They both looked very hard at the little brown door in the hedge bank.

A few moments later the door opened, and the mole came out holding a small glass jar containing some blue powder.

In a flash, the mole opened the jar and sprinkled some of the powder onto each of the children.

Almost straight away both the children found themselves shrinking very fast. The fallen leaves and twigs around them became very big and the hedge bank became huge.

In a moment the children were the same size as the mole, who was standing beside them and smiling from ear to ear.

"Hello," said the mole, "now I can see that you are the children who I have met before."

Ben and Sue both became very excited, for not only were they the same size as the mole, but they could also understand what he was saying.

"Yes we are," Sue replied, "and you are Mr Arthur Mole," she continued with a huge smile on her face.

The children had met Mr Arthur Mole and his friends before. That is when they saw lots of magic happen in the Fairy Wood.

Mr Mole invited the children to go through the open door and into the hedge bank. The children followed Mr Mole through the door, only to find the familiar sight of Mrs Mole standing beside the glowing fire, with her apron around her waist and her hat upon her head. She had a broad welcoming smile on her face when she saw the children.

Closing the door, Mr Mole told the children how good it was to see them again.Ben thought it was time to tell Mr and Mrs Mole the reason they have come to find them. He wasted no time in telling them what they had heard their father and his manager talking about. He told them that the hedge bank may be dug up to make larger fields.

"Oh dear, oh dear, oh dear," said Mr Mole with his forehead resting in his paw, "this is a very serious situation and must be dealt with straight away."

Chapter 2
Find the Wood Elders

Mr Mole stood with his back towards the fire, warming his black velvet trousers, and thought very hard.

"Mrs Mole my dear, could you please find Mr Wood the mouse and Walter Vole and ask them to come for a meeting straight away? Oh, I think we should also try to find Mr Red the squirrel, I think he will be very useful."

Mrs Mole made sure her hat was firmly in place on her head; she opened the back door, and was gone in a flash.

Mr Mole said he was not a good host, as he had forgotten to ask the children to sit down. He arranged some chairs around the fire and invited the children to sit on them.

Mr Mole walked up and down in front of the fire, with his paws clasped firmly behind his back and his head bowed, for what seemed to be a long time. Eventually the back door opened, and in came Walter Vole followed by Mr Wood the mouse and Mrs Mole. They were all out of breath, as they had been in a hurry to come to the meeting.

"I can't find Mr Red the squirrel," said Mrs Mole in a very out-of-breath way, "I have looked everywhere but I can't find him," she said as she sat down very heavily in a soft armchair.

"That's all right," said Mr Mole, "We can find him later, but now we must decide what to do about our problem."

On the way home Mrs Mole had told the others what the problem was all about. This saved a lot of time when they arrived at the meeting.

"I think we must all move to the river," said Walter Vole, finding a chair to sit on.

"That is not fair," said Mr Wood the mouse, "you usually live in the water all the time, I can't swim and I hate the water. What about all the other animals that live in the hedgerows? No, I can't do that."

"Please do not panic over this," said Mr Mole, "I think we should tell the Wood Elders about the problem, and ask them to help us."

"What a very good idea my dear," said Mrs Mole standing beside her husband for support.

So it was decided, they must find the Wood Elders as soon as possible and ask for advice.

"We must leave right now as time is short," said Mr Mole.

Mrs Mole stood in front of her husband and said, "You are not leaving me behind this time, I always have to hear about your adventures when it is all over, and you have returned home. The children are staying with my sister so I am coming with you as well."

"Very well," said Mr Mole, "the more help we have the better."

Mr. Mole made sure the fire was put out in the fire grate, that all the candles were blown out, and that the front door was locked. Mrs Mole opened the back door and went through it followed by Mr Wood the mouse, Walter Vole, Sue, Ben and finally Mr Mole who locked the door behind them.

They entered a well-lit staircase going down. The steps were worn smooth from frequent use. The walls and roof were made of soil, with the ends of tree and plant roots showing through. The tunnel was lit at regular intervals by glowworms lying on the floor beside the walls.

This was a different route to the one taken on a previous time, as this tunnel went down, and not as previously when it was level.

"We must go down to the earth works," said Mr Mole leading the way. "It is a long way down."

The steps seemed to go down for ever. At last they were in a large hall.

The hall was full of tables, with lots of elves working away at them. None of the elves even noticed the visitors to the hall.

"What are they all doing" asked Ben, who was holding Sue very close to his side.

"They are weeding," said Mr Mole, "humans always plant good seeds to grow, but weeds must grow as well. If they do not grow, the whole balance of the plants, and the air we that breathe will change. So it is their job to make sure we have enough weeds to balance the plants that grow. They make sure the weeds are in good condition for the elves to plant during the night."

"So that is why weeds appear to pop up over night," remarked Sue with an understanding look on her face.

Mr Mole led the group of animals and children to the other side of the hall, where a large wooden door was closed in front of them. Mr Mole knocked very hard three times on the door, then stood away from the door and waited.

After a few seconds a deep voice from behind the door said, "Come in."

Mr Mole opened the door and went in, followed by all the animals and children.

Sat in a large chair with its back to the door was something. The something had bright green hair and a pink cape.

"Shut the door please," said the something. So Mrs Mole closed the door behind her with a loud 'click'.

"Who are you?" asked the something.

"I am Arthur Mole with some friends."

"Oh Arthur Mole," said the something as it stood up, swishing its cape around. As it did so the cape became tangled in a hatstand that stood beside the chair, the stand whizzed at high speed across the room just missing Walter Vole. It stopped on the edge of a table, balancing as if not knowing which way to fall. While this was happening the something flew across the room very quickly, and stood in front of the hat stand shaking its finger at it, as if telling it off.

The hat stand appeared to be moving its arms as if in a dance. The something then pointed to where the hat stand had been standing in the first place.

The something said in a stern voice, "Go."

The hat stand jumped off the table and appeared to walk, very slowly, with its head bowed, to the position indicated by the something.

In a deep voice the something said, "Hello, I am Witch Clumsy – oh dear I am clumsy all of the time. How can I help you?"

Witch Clumsy was indeed clumsy, for as she turned to face her guests, she tripped over her pink cape and only just managed to hold onto her bright yellow cat.

She smiled at the animals and children, and flashed her bright red eyes, and twitched her upturned long nose.

Mr Mole explained to Witch Clumsy about the problem with the hedge banks.

The witch sat down again in her chair, and as she did so the others heard the air whizzing out of the cushion.

"I will set a spell on the farmer to make him change his mind," said the witch, "but I am very likely to make a mistake, so a spell must be done another way."

Ben started to say, "Please don't set a spell on our Fa–"

But he was stopped very quickly by Mr. Mole who said. "Yes we must find another way."

The witch then continued to say, "I agree that you must ask the Wood Elders for help. I can help you on your way by showing you the right road to take. When you leave this room by the other door, you will find yourselves in a room with no door. You must all close your eyes, and say together 'up', you will then find yourselves on the right road. Keep going until your path is blocked, then follow the next instructions."

The witch stood up again, and as she did so a very large button on her cape caught in the arm of her chair, With a loud 'POP' the button came off her cape, and shot across the room at great speed. It bounced off a saucepan resting on a shelf with a 'PING', it sped across the room in the other direction, until it hit a frying pan hanging on the wall with a 'BOING', The button continued to fly at high speed backwards, and forwards, across the room, banging off articles just like the ball in a game of tennis.

"STOP!" shouted the witch as she ducked under the flying button again.

By this time all the others were lying flat on the floor, covering their heads with their paws and hands.

"Wow," said Mr Wood the mouse, as they all got back onto their feet.

Without another word, they all went through the other door and as described by the witch, found themselves in a well-lit room with no door.

All of the friends looked around the room, and then at one another. There was indeed no door at all; even the door they had just come through had disappeared.

Mrs Mole then reminded everybody that the witch had said that they must close their eyes and say 'up' to get out of the room. So they all stood in a circle and held hands and paws in a ring, closed their eyes, and together in a firm voice, they all said 'up.' In a flash the roof of the room opened and they were all travelling upwards very fast. The wind passing them was very strong, and was making Mr Walter Vole's and Mr Wood the mouse's ears push flat against their heads.

At last they could smell the outside air, and with a *thud* they all found themselves sitting on the grass, with no hole in the ground to be seen.

"Wow," said Ben standing up, "That was different," he added.

Everyone stood up and looked around. They were on a grassed area beside a narrow pathway. The path seemed to lead into a wood in one direction, and a very steep hill in the other.

"I think we should go along the path towards the wood," said Mr Wood the mouse, "it looks a lot easier than the other way," he continued.

"I agree," said Walter Vole.

So, all six of the animals and children started to walk along the path, and into the wood. It seemed like a 'nice' wood, with the blue sky above, the birds singing, and the woodland smells of wild garlic in the air.

They started talking amongst themselves about the silly things that Witch Clumsy had been doing, and laughing about her mistakes. As they were walking and talking, nobody had noticed that the wood had changed, and that there were very high rock walls on both sides of the path. The path became very narrow. They were all prevented from going forward, by a large rock in the middle of the path, blocking their way.

"Oh dear," said Mrs Mole, "I don't think I could climb over that."

"You don't have to," returned a voice.

"Who said that?" Mr Mole asked, looking around.

"It was me," was the reply again.

The rock was like any other rock, it had lumps and dips all over it, and it had a large amount of moss on the top. The moss looked like hair, thought Sue, when gradually the lumps and dips in the rock started to change.

Firstly two eyes appeared in the dips, then a nose on a lump, and a mouth on another lump, with a huge smile.

Everyone took a step backwards, as they did not expect that to happen.

Mrs Mole told everybody that she was very frightened and did not like being in this place.

"Hello, my name is Kilo," said the stone in a very deep voice. "When I was small I only weighed a few grams, so they called me Gram, but now that I am big they call me Kilo. I don't like being big, as I can't roll around as I used to, so I have gathered moss on my head. I was told that a rolling stone gathers no moss. That is true you know. Oh, I am very sorry. I think I am boring you."

The rock stopped talking at last, and just sat in the path, with a wide smile on his face.

"We were told to travel along the path by Witch Clumsy, until we were stopped, we then have to follow the next instructions," said Mr Mole to the rock. The rock seemed to be looking straight past everyone and into the distance.

"Are you expecting anyone else?" said Kilo the rock.

Everyone turned around, and there, running along the path was Mr Red the squirrel.

"Wait for me!" he shouted as he came towards the others. He screeched to a halt, and did not appear to be out of breath at all.

"I say, Witch Clumsy is a bit different, she turned me into a rabbit because she thought my front teeth looked like a rabbit, so the rest of me should look like a rabbit. Took a bit of speed to get out of that one, I ended up chasing her yellow cat, so she had to change me back into a squirrel to slow me down. Sorry if I am late, as I have been making a map, to remind me where I have buried my nuts. Oh, who is that?" said Mr Red the squirrel, looking at Kilo the rock.

"This is Kilo the rock," said Mr Mole, "he is in our way at the moment."

"Am I in the way?" Kilo asked. "Oh I am sorry. If one of you would tap me on the head three times, I think things would be different."

Mr Red the squirrel pushed through the others, and tapped the rock tree times on the head. Straight away a very loud noise came from inside the rock, and it was changing shape all the time. After a few noisy moments, the rock had changed into a very strange creature that still looked a bit like a rock, but it had short arms, and short fat legs. The smiling mouth had changed into a mouth with large lips, and dribble hanging out of each side. He was now a lot smaller than the rock.

Everyone looked at the creature with their mouths open, feeling astonished at the change that had happened.

"I am sorry if I frighten you," said the creature, "it is only because of the way people see me, I am still nice inside, just because I do not look nice outside, does not mean that I am not nice inside," he said. "At least I am not now blocking your way. I am still Kilo, but I have changed into a troll. But I am a good troll. I am not like some of my cousins. I can now help you to move on. You have to walk on the air, take one step forward, and two steps backwards."

As the troll finished his instructions, there was again a loud noise, and the troll turned back into a rock again, but this time it was a small rock, and only blocked part of the path.

Chapter 3
Fairy Rings

One by one, the animals and children squeezed past the now silent rock, and started to walk along the path. The problem was that nobody could walk forward. Every time a step was taken forward, two steps were taken backwards. As a result everyone was crashing into one another until Mr Walter Vole said very loudly, "Stop walking."

Everybody stopped and looked at one another. Mr Mole was standing on Mr Wood the mouse's tail, Mrs Mole was standing on Mr Red the squirrel's tail, Ben was rolling around on the floor, and Sue was laughing at everyone.

"It's not funny," said Mr Red the squirrel, shaking the dust off his bushy tail.

Ben suggested that they all turn around, and walked backwards.

"That's a good idea," said Mr Mole.

So they all turned around and started to walk backwards. It worked, for as each step was taken forward, two steps were taken backwards. In a very funny fashion, they progressed along the pathway.

They had only taken a few steps when Ben noticed that none their feet were touching the ground at all.

"Are we flying?" Sue asked, as she seemed to be pedalling in mid air.

"Yes we are flying," replied Mrs Mole, beginning to lose her balance, and holding Mr Mole's arm.

"The rock did say we had to walk on the air. I think we should take much bigger steps," said Ben.

"It's all very well for you," said Mr Wood the mouse, "I have only got short legs."

"And so have I," added Walter Vole.

"Let's take a rest," insisted Mrs Mole, trying to sit on the ground, but still being pushed upwards into the air.

It was at that moment when they noticed a circle of dust on the ground, underneath them.

The dust circle became very dusty, with a blue glow coming from underneath the dust. Faint chattering could be heard, coming from the dust circle.

"What is that?" Sue asked, looking very hard at the blue glow on the ground.

"That is a fairy ring being made," said Mr Mole, "the problem is that the fairies are trying to make the ring in the wrong place. If they made the ring in the field it would show as a dark ring on the grass. But on a dusty path, all that will happen is lots of dust, and no marks will be seen afterwards. They are dancing in a circle very fast, and that is what makes the dust."

Sue was about to ask another question, when all of a sudden the dust stopped, and four fairies were seen standing where the circle had been. They were chatting to one another very fast with squeaky voices, and their wings were still fluttering.

"Hello," said Mrs Mole. The fairies looked all around them wondering who had spoken to them.

"We are up here," continued Mrs Mole, "up here in the air."

All four fairies looked up, and almost jumped out of their skins when they saw the animals and children floating in the air above them.

"Can you please help us we are stuck, up here in the air, and cannot get down?" Mrs Mole asked, in a very soft voice, hoping not to sound too frightened.

All four fairies started laughing very loudly, and were rolling around on the floor, holding their tummies as they laughed, but taking care not to damage their wings.

"You must have met Witch Clumsy, and Kilo the rock. Everybody ends up in the air after meeting them," said one of the fairies, as she tried to control her laughter.

All four fairies looked at one another and whispered some words that nobody else understood. They all stretched their arms in the air. All of a sudden, all of the animals and children fell to the ground, with some falling upon others, and others landing on heads, arms and legs, all of them in a jumble on the floor.

The fairies looked at the pile of bodies on the floor, and continued laughing with their hands over their mouth's, to hide their laughter.

Mr Mole was the first to stand up. He made himself stand very tall, and brushed his velvet coat with his paws. All the others slowly stood up, shaking, and brushing the dust from them.

At last the fairies managed to stop laughing.

"Where are you trying to go?" the tallest of the fairies asked in a very soft voice, still with a smile on her face.

"We have a problem in our part of the wood," replied Mr Mole, who seemed to have taken charge of the situation. "We are trying to reach the Wood Elders, to see if they can help us," he continued.

"There are several Wood Elders," said the tall fairy, "there is the Old Owl, Walt the Wizard and Tommy the

Toad. They are the Wood Elders. Oh yes, there is also Witch Forgetful, the problem with Witch Forgetful is that she has forgotten she is a Wood Elder, but she is nice. Which Wood Elder do you want to see, as they each live in a different part of the wood?"

Mr Mole explained to the fairy the problem they have with the farmer, and the hedge bank.

"I don't know who would be the best Wood Elder to help you," said the tall fairy.

The fairy then appeared to be having a conversation with the other fairies in a very fast, and a very soft voice, but nobody could understand what they were saying.

"We think you must visit all of them in turn, to find out which of them can help you. It might be best to visit Tommy the toad first as he is the nearest. You will find him in his house of soggy leaves, near the bottom of his tree, beside the smelly bog. To get there, you must each have some fairy dust with you in your pockets. I don't mean the sparkly type, but real dust made by fairies. We will run around in a circle and make some dust, like we did before, when you see the dust rise, grab some with your hand and put it in your pocket,"

The fairies began to walk in a circle, and then run in a circle until they were running so fast it was impossible to see them. As they ran the dust began to rise from the floor. Each of the children and animals grabbed at the dust with their hands and paws. They put the collected dust in their pockets. The fairies stopped running, and the dust settled on the floor again.

"Just walk along this path until you meet Nobby the gnome. He will be able to tell you were Tommy the toad is, as he does travel about from place to place," said the tall fairy.

Then, with a very gentle flutter of wings, all four fairies flew off into the distance, still chattering at high speed.

"I have never seen fairies like that before," said Sue, "I have seen them in books, but I have never seen a real one before. That was fantastic."

Mr Red the squirrel, being a little put out that Mr Mole appeared to be taking the lead, said, "I think we had better move off along the path, it looks like we have a lot to do before we will get an answer to our problem."

Walter Vole pushed past everybody, to walk in front saying, "I can smell water, just what I need."

The group moved along the path, chatting amongst themselves all the way. They never did find Nobby the gnome, so they continued along the path. By now, the high banks on each side of the path had gone, and had been replaced by the trees and bushes of a wood. The air was fresh, and the clear blue sky could be seen through the canopy of tree leaves above.

As the trees became fewer, the air changed to a funny smell. It was rather like a smell of bad eggs. Mr Wood the mouse was the first to reach the banks of a very muddy pond. The pond was surrounded by broken down, rotting trees and overhanging branches, with the ends of most of the branches covered by the water. Broken branches littered the pond, and the bad smell was now very strong.

"Wow, what a pong," said Mr Wood the mouse holding his nose.

"Lovely," Walter Vole said, looking very longing at the water.

Mrs Mole sat on a rock beside the pond, to get her breath back after the walk.

The two children just stood on the edge of the pond, trying not to get their feet wet.

Mr Mole started to investigate. He moved to the left around the pond, while Mr Red the squirrel started to walk to the right around the pond.

Ben pulled at Sue's sleeve, and pointed to a large ripple appearing in the middle of the pond.

"Is it a crocodile?" Sue asked. She was looking very worried.

"I don't think so," said Ben not sounding too sure, "I don't think crocodiles live around here."

Mrs Mole had already seen the ripple, and was shouting to her husband, to warn him.

"Arthur," she shouted pointing to the pond, "Arthur, look at the wave in the pond."

As Mrs Mole was saying the words, there was an enormous splash of water in front of her. She could not believe her eyes, for stood in front of her, was a large otter, standing on his back legs, and using his tail to balance himself.

"What are you doing disturbing my peace and quiet? I had just chosen a fish to catch, when I saw you. I am very cross, as I now have to try to remember which fish I had chosen."

By this time Mr Mole and Mr Red the squirrel had returned to the others, beside the pond.

Mr Red the squirrel stood very tall on his hind legs, and appeared to be boxing the otter with his short front legs as he said, "We are only trying to find Tommy the toad, who is a Wood Elder. We did not disturb you as much as you frightened us."

"Will you all please calm down," said Mr Arthur Mole, trying to be sensible. He continued, "We have a very big problem in our part of the wood."

He explained the problem with the hedge bank, and the farmer wanting to dig it up.

"Oh dear," said the otter, with an understanding look on his face. "We had a similar problem here in our pond, a while ago. The farmer in this part of the wood did not like me making dams with mud, as I flooded his fields. But they dug a new river beside the pond, so the water could pass by, and not flood the field. That's why the pond is now very smelly, because the water in it does not move. We were very worried at the time, so I do understand your problem."

Mr Red the squirrel stopped the boxing movements with his front legs and sat upright, with his tail balancing him.

"Do you know where Tommy the Toad is?" Ben asked, very slowly, as this was the first time he had ever had a conversation with a live otter.

"Tommy lives on a small dry patch in the middle of the pond, beyond the tree branches that I have piled up to make a nest for myself," replied the otter.

Mrs Mole stood up, and said to the otter. "As you can see, it is very important we see the toad. Is there a dry way that we can reach him?"

"Those of you who cannot swim can ride on my back if you like, but I can only take two at a time," replied the otter.

"Thank you very much," said Ben.

The otter slid the front half of his body into the water. Mr and Mrs Mole were the first to climb onto his back.

"Hold on tight," said the otter. A push with his hind legs and they were off across the smelly pond. Walter Vole could not wait any longer. He ran, very fast into the pond. He dived under the water, and popped up a little way away, with his head looking through the surface weed. He dived again, with his rear feet and his tail the last to disappear under the water. Moments later he came to the surface again, and floated on his back on the water with his feet in the air.

"This is more like it," said Walter Vole, floating on his back with his front paws behind his head, as if he was sun bathing.

"Why don't you go onto the island, and find Tommy the toad," shouted Ben to Walter Vole.

Walter Vole looked at Ben, put his thumb in the air, and disappeared under the water again.

By this time, the otter had landed Mr and Mrs Mole on the island, and was now returning at high speed under the water. He came out of the water again, in front of the children, Mr Wood the mouse and Mr Red the squirrel. He stood on the bank with his four paws spread out, and shook his body very hard, just like a dog when it is wet. Water splashed everywhere, and everybody had to take a few steps backwards very quickly to avoid the splashes.

"Who's next?" he asked.

Ben and Sue quickly jumped onto the otter's back, and held on very tightly to his fur. In a moment, the otter was into the water again, and moving very quickly, without any effort. When they reached the island, the children jumped off the otter's back. The otter disappeared under the water again, to collect the others.

Chapter 4

Mr Fox Helps

The dry patch in the middle of the pond was covered with old leaves, broken sticks, moss and general woodland rubbish.

Walter Vole waddled out of the water with a large smile on his face, just as the otter came on land, with Mr Wood the mouse and Mr Red the squirrel, hanging onto his fur so tightly that it made the otter shout out very loud. "Please get off my back you are pulling my fur too tightly!"

"Sorry," said Mr Red the squirrel, "we can't swim, and we hate the water, we don't want to drown you know."

Both of them jumped off the otter's back, and joined the others on the dry patch.

"I must try to remember which fish I was going to catch before I met you," said the otter, as he turned around and slid into the water. In a moment he was gone.

"How are we going to get off this island now?" Mr Wood the mouse asked, looking around for a means of a dry escape.

"Something will turn up," said Mr Mole, with some confidence.

All the friends looked around for the pile of soggy leaves where they were told that Tommy the toad lived, but there was no obvious pile of leaves, so they all started to search the leaves in front of them as they walked, turning them over with their feet.

Mrs Mole eventually sat down on a broken-down log to rest, when she heard in front of her, a very funny voice saying, "What are you looking for?"

The voice sounded very much as though its owner, was drinking a glass of water at the same time as talking.

"Where are you, and who are you?" she shouted, as she stood up holding the bottom of her skirts above her feet, so that she could see more clearly what was on the floor.

The leaves parted right in front of her, and there she saw a pair of bright yellow eyes, looking up at her.

"It's me Tommy the toad," came the watery reply.

First one leg, with a big flat foot appeared, then another, and with a huge explosion of the leaves, the toad revealed himself, blinking his large yellow eyes, at Mrs Mole.

"Don't wink at me Mr Toad, I'm already married," said Mrs Mole, as she took a step backwards.

By this time, the others had heard what was going on, and surrounded the toad. The toad turned around to see all of the others looking at him.

“How did you all get here? I thought I was a long way away from everybody else, except for Sky the fox, and myself,” said the toad.

“Is there a fox here as well?” Mr Red the squirrel asked, in a very shaky voice.

“Oh he’s all right, as long as he is not hungry,” said the toad, “he doesn’t like me, as he tried to eat my friend, but toads don’t taste very nice. Oh, by the way, I’m Tommy the toad, and I was not winking at you,” he continued, looking at Mrs Mole.

Mr Mole stepped forward, and said to Tommy, “Pleased to meet you. We are here because we have a problem in our part of the wood. We were told you could help us as you are a Wood Elder.”

Mr Mole continued to tell Tommy the story of the problem, and how they all had arrived at where they were, and all of the creatures they had met on the way.

"You must be very tired," said Tommy, "I would invite you to eat, but I only eat slugs, and I don't think you would like that. You need help from someone who can think, and move fast. I am a bit slow, as I can only hop around with my big tummy. You need to talk to the Old Owl. He is very clever, and can move very fast. I will arrange for some help to get you there."

Tommy the toad took a large, deep breath; as he did so a very large bag appeared under his chin, full of air. He lifted his large knobbly head, opened his mouth, and the loudest croak that was ever heard came out of his mouth.

"While we wait for a reply, could somebody please scratch the back of my neck?" Tommy asked. "I just can't reach that part, and it's been itching for months."

Walter Vole moved forward to scratch the toad. "Oh thanks," said the toad. "One day I will be able to return the favour, when you just don't expect it."

Suddenly, there was a noise coming from inside a nearby bush. A long nose appeared from the bush, twitched, and then, followed by the head, and then the whole, of a very handsome, brown and white fox.

"Hi, I'm Sky the fox," said the fox, with a very big grin on his face, and a sidewise glance at all the animals and children.

“I should have been called Sly the fox, but they spelt it wrong on my birth certificate, so I am Sky.” The fox was looking at each of the group in turn and thinking to himself, what do they taste like?

Tommy the toad asked the fox to take the group to the Old Owl, by the most direct route, and to keep them all safe, as they had very important business, to help to protect Fairy Wood.

The fox agreed, and led everybody into the bush that he had come from earlier.

They all said goodbye to the toad, and followed the fox into the bush.

Once inside the bush, the fox led them into a large hole in the ground, just large enough for the fox. As the others were smaller than the fox, there was plenty of room for them.

The fox ran on and on along the tunnel, sometimes looking back, to make sure they were all following, with that sly smile still on his face.

All of the followers were very concerned about the fox, as they all knew he would enjoy eating any of them, given the chance, but he did promise the toad to keep them all safe.

At last the fox slowed down, turned around, put his paw to his mouth as if to ask for silence, and crept forward, with the group of friends creeping, slowly behind.

"This is it," whispered Mr Wood the mouse to Walter Vole, "our time is up. I knew we should not have trusted a fox."

The procession slowed to almost a stop when the fox, pointed to a cavern in the side of the tunnel. The cavern was lined with straw.

"Too far to run now," continued Mr Wood the mouse, "can't escape; nowhere to go; this is really it; goodbye my friend."

As they all passed the cavern, they were astonished to see another fox curled up as if asleep, with four small cubs cuddled to the side of the sleeping fox.

"That's the family," whispered Sky the fox, as he took a lasting glance at the sleeping group.

"Phew," said Mr Wood the mouse wiping his forehead with the back of his paw. "I thought he was getting ready to eat us."

After passing the foxes' den, with the sleeping fox and cubs, Sky the fox increased his speed again, along the passages. He continued to glance behind him as he travelled, along with that hungry look on his face.

At last the air became fresher again, with a spark of sunlight in the distance.

The group following the fox were very glad to know they were close to the outside, even Mr and Mrs Mole, who were used to being underground.

The fox squeezed though the last part of the tunnel towards the outside. He put his nose in the air, and took a deep breath.

"Please move along Mr Fox," said Mrs Mole, pushing the fox forward, "we all want some fresh air."

The fox moved out of the hole, followed quickly by all the others. Everybody took deep breaths, and sat on the floor around the hole.

Mr Wood the mouse was watching a worm in front of him with interest as he rested. The worm was halfway buried in the ground, and half above the surface, looking around.

Everyone felt a big draught of wind, and a large black, male, blackbird landed beside Mr Wood the mouse. The mouse ran to hide behind Mr Mole, as he knew some bids liked mice to eat. The bird was not interested in the mouse at all; instead, he grabbed the worm with his beak, and pulled very hard. His feet were firmly on the ground, and his body leaned backwards as he pulled.

At last, the worm 'popped' out of the ground, and the bird flew off with it in its beak. The draught of wind from its wings made a huge dust.

"That was close," said Mr Wood the mouse, appearing from behind Mr Mole, where he had been hiding, and wiping his brow with the back of his paw again.

Chapter 5

Advice from the Owl

Sky the fox stopped smelling the air, and said that he knew where the King Oak tree was from here. He then said that the Old Wise Owl lived inside the tree.

The fox continued to lead the group along a path, through a different part of the wood. At last, in front of the group, was a very large, old oak tree.

"This is King Oak," said Sky the fox. "I will wait here until you are all inside, before I go. I promised Tommy the toad to keep you safe this time, but I might prefer to eat you next time,"

Everyone looked at one another, and wondered what he meant by the last thing he said.

The fox knocked hard on the side of the tree with his paw.

A door in the side of the tree opened. The fox ran off into the wood looking behind him as he ran with a sly smile on his face.

The door was opened wide, with a 'creek'. A badger was standing in the doorway, with a big smile on his face. He was wearing a long butler's coat, and a bow tie.

"Please come in and follow me," said the badger.

The group went through the door. Once inside the tree the friends could not believe their eyes. They were in a very large hall. The floor was made of marble stone, the ceiling was very high and being supported by carved stone columns.

The badger asked them to follow him down a staircase. They all followed the badger down the stairs, until they came to another hall. There were a number of closed doors in the walls.

The badger knocked on one of the doors, and a voice from inside said, "Come in please."

The badger opened the door, and the group went into the room.

Once inside the room, they saw a very large and very black crow, standing on the back of a wonderful carved wooden chair. The crow had a golden book tucked under one wing.

The chair was at one end of a very large wooden table, with other chairs placed around the table.

The crow said, "Welcome, can I help you?"

"We are looking for the Old Wise Owl, who is the Wood Elder," said Mr Red the squirrel, looking at the crow with amazement. The crow was peering through a pair of spectacles, placed on the end of his beak. He was obviously having problems seeing through them, as he was looking and talking to a chair on the other side of the room, and not at Mr Red the squirrel.

Mrs Mole said, "Can you see us Mr Crow?"

"Is there more than one of you?" the crow asked.

"Yes, there are seven of us!" shouted Walter Vole.

The crow did not know which way to look, as there were voices coming from every direction. At last the crow took off the spectacles, with a blink of his eyes and said. "Oh there you are. I have borrowed these spectacles from the Wise Old Owl as he is not here at the moment. I thought they would make me look wise as well. I don't think it worked, I really don't look wise at all."

Mr Mole was the first to speak, "We were hoping that the Wise Old Owl would be here, we have a big problem, and we need his help."

"He has gone to visit his sister who has just hatched twins," replied the crow, as he jumped from the back of the chair, and onto the table. "He might be back at any time, or he may not. He did not say how long he will be. Can I give him a message?"

The Old Crow put the golden book down, and started to march up and down on the table, with his wings behind his back, and his beak in the air, trying to look important.

"Do you know where his sister is nesting?" Mrs Mole asked, in a motherly sort of way.

"Don't know," replied the crow, still marching up and down on the table.

There were a few papers on the table with lots of writing on them. Walter Vole was trying to read what was on them, with his head almost upside down.

Without any warning, the door at the end of the room opened wide. There was a huge gust of wind. The papers took off from the table and blew across the room. A very large owl flew into the room. It flew low over the group, and landed on the back of the chair that the crow had been standing on.

The owl tucked his wings away, one by one, and hopped onto the seat of the chair.

The animals and children were astonished, and each took a step backwards.

The crow stopped marching around. He quickly picked up the golden book, and placed it on the table in front of the owl. He looked at the group, with his head leaning to one side.

"Whooo let youuu in tooo the meeting roooom?" asked the owl.

"It was the Badger butler," Mr Red the squirrel replied, "why are you talking in that funny way?"

"Oh, I am sorry," the owl said, "I have been spending too much time with my sister, and other owls. This is how they all speak you know. Why do you want to see me?"

Mrs Mole sat on the chair beside the owl, and told him the whole story, from start to finish without stopping. When she had finished telling the owl about the problem, the owl nodded his head, and appeared to smile at Mrs Mole.

"I have come across this problem before," said the owl, "but on that occasion we were not in time to save the hedge bank. We have to work quickly this time."

"We seem to have taken a very long time getting this far," said Sue, "our mother and father will be very worried that we have been away for so long."

“Please do not be worried about that,” said the owl, “for Fairy Wood is magic, as you have already found out. For what seems to be an hour in Fairy Wood, is only one minute in your world. You will not be missed.”

Sue felt very relieved by what the owl had said.

The Wise Old Owl picked up the spectacles that the crow had been wearing, and put them on the end of his beak. He sat still in his chair for some time, thinking, with his wings resting on the table, and his eyes closed. The others started to become board with waiting, so they started to look around the room. The crow was still sitting on the back of a chair, looking at the owl, and not moving. It was a big room, with long curtains from ceiling to floor. There were several doors around the room, all of them closed. The ceiling was covered in a silk material that was hanging in loops.

Everyone jumped when the owl said, "We need the help of a witch, but I do not know which witch to ask. Crow, please pass me the golden book?"

The crow jumped down from his perch, and hopped over the table to the owl. He placed the book, very carefully in front of the owl, and opened it to the first page.

The owl, pushed his spectacles further back onto his beak, and started very gently to turn the pages.

Every so often, the owl would stop, and look at a page, and say, "maybe," or "I wonder;" or "defiantly not."

The owl stopped at a page, and said in a very loud voice, "Yes."

Mr Red the squirrel had been standing near the owl. He noticed that on the pages were pictures of witches, with very funny writing underneath each picture.

"This is the one," said the owl in an excited voice, "Are we all ready?"

Ready for what, thought Ben?

The owl looked at everybody in the room in turn, he then touched the picture with the end of his wing. He muttered the words that were written in the book, under the picture.

Nothing happened. The owl looked at the crow; the crow looked at the owl; the children looked at each other, and Mr Mole asked, "What was supposed to happen?"

The owl looked at the book again. A moment later, he smiled and said, "I forgot to press the button."

The owl touched a red dot on the page with the end of his wing, and before anybody could blink, the room started to shake like an earthquake. The table started to jump about as if it was dancing, the long curtains shook and the chairs moved around the floor. All was then still again as quickly as it has started, but nothing had changed, there was not a witch in the room. Everyone looked at the Old Owl. Mrs Mole was just about to speak when there was a large *thud* under the table, and somebody said, "Ouch."

The voice came from under the table. Moments later, a very beautiful lady crawled out from under the table, on her hands and knees. She slowly stood beside the table, and straightened her long flowing blue skirts with her hands.

Mr Red the squirrel noticed how beautiful she was. Her hands were very long and slender with lovely nails, she had long red hair, and a slim elegant body. His head leaned to one side, his eyes opened wide, and his mouth fell open; he thought he was in love.

The beautiful woman moved very gracefully to the far end of the table. She stopped, and turned to face the others in the room.

The beautiful lady said in a in a very soft, but firm voice, “Hello, I am Witch... Oh dear, I have forgotten who I am. Oh yes,” she continued, “I am Witch Forgetful. Fancy me forgetting my own name. I shall forget who I am, next.”

Mr Mole, stood in front of the beautiful witch, and in a trembling voice, asked, “Can you please help us, we need to save our hedge bank from being dug up, to make bigger fields. We don’t know how to save our homes from being destroyed.”

The witch took a pencil, and notebook, from under her skirts, licked the end of the pencil, and said, “This sounds important, so I think I should write everything down in my notebook. I have a terrible memory. This is the curse of being a witch. You either look terrible, or you are nasty, or stupid, or forgetful like me, there is always something wrong with us. I am very thankful that I only have a bad memory. Please tell me again, so that I do not miss anything?”

Mr Mole repeated the whole story, with frequent interruptions from Mrs Mole, and Walter Vole. The witch wrote everything down in her notebook.

As she turned the page in her notebook, the witch stopped writing, put her hand over here mouth, and took in a deep breath, her beautiful blue eyes open wide.

“I should be at the spells meeting, and I have forgotten. I have it written in my notebook, but I forgot to look this morning. I really must not miss the meeting, as I am supposed to be explaining how some new spells work. There is no other way, you must all come with me then I will be able to help you.”

The animals and children started to complain about having to go with the witch. The Wise Old Owl became very excited, and said, “If you want help, then you must go with Witch Forgetful, You must trust her.”

“Follow me,” said the witch. She snapped her thumb and middle finger together, and she was gone; none of the others disappeared; they were all in the same places, as they were before the witch had vanished.

All of a sudden the witch was standing next to the table again. She said to the group, "I am very sorry, I had forgotten to tell you how to follow me. This time, I want you all to look very hard into my eyes. I hope it will work this time."

So, everybody looked very hard into the lovely blue eyes of the witch. Nobody noticed that they had left the owl's room until they all found themselves in a very large cave. The cave was lit by lots of fires burning in open containers, with the flames flashing and darting about, making odd shadows on the walls of the cave.

Chapter 6
The Spells Meeting

The group of animals and children were amazed at the spectacle that surrounded them. There were lots of fairies and elves running around, looking as if they were very busy carrying out tasks. There were a number of gnomes, but most of them were either sitting, or lying down looking very lazy. All of the gnomes were very fat. There was one gnome, sitting beside a small pond, with a fishing rod. Ben thought he had seen him before somewhere. There were a large number and variety of witches. There were big ones, small ones, fat ones, thin ones, ugly ones, pretty ones, quiet and noisy ones. Some had very bright clothes, while others had drab clothes. Most of them were very busy doing something, or talking to someone else.

Mr Mole pointed out Witch Clumsy amongst the group, she kept tripping over her cape. Witch Big Feet was there as well; she had very big feet herself, and was looking at everybody else's feet. There was the Wet Witch, she was dripping wet, and leaving a pool of water wherever she went. The Which Witch was looking in every direction she could. She is the witch that does not know which way to go. She looks in one direction, and walks in another, so she was bumping into things and people.

All of the activities around the group of animals and children were very busy, and very noisy. Nobody was taking any notice of the group that had just arrived. Witch Forgetful had disappeared among the other witches.

Sue started to walk around, looking at her surroundings. There were things, and people, she had never seen before. All over the cave there were large spikes of what looked like rock, either standing on the ground pointing upwards, or from the ceiling hanging down.

"What are these?" Sue asked Ben.

"They are stalagmites and stalactites," replied Ben to his sister. "The ones coming down are called stalactites, and the ones growing out of the floor are stalagmites. The easy way to remember is that mites run around the floor, so stalagmites are the ones on the floor."

The light from the many fires made the spikes flash with colour, and gave strange shadows on the walls.

Mr Wood the mouse was hiding behind Mr Red the squirrel. Walter Vole had his paws over his ears because of the loud noise. Mrs Mole held her husband's paw very tightly, as she was very frightened.

The beautiful Witch Forgetful appeared from nowhere, and was standing in front of the friends.

"I'm very sorry," she said, "I forgot why I was here, and that I had brought you with me. I have to go and meet another witch for a while, but I cannot remember who she is, or where I have to meet her. Why don't you look around, until I return, if I remember?"

Witch Forgetful took her notebook out of her pocket, opened the book, and after reading the writing on the page, she smiled, and gently floated away into the darkness.

Mrs Mole felt a little better after seeing the lovely witch again, so with interest on her face, she started to investigate the cave.

Mr Red the squirrel found he had a very wet tail. “Must have been the Wet Witch,” he muttered to himself, trying hard to shake off the water.

A very bright yellow cat ran in front of Mr Mole, followed by Witch Clumsy, running, and tripping over her cape again and again. She caught the cat as she fell to the ground, right in front of Sue. Sue looked in amazement at the witch, who was lying on the floor, and looking up at her with big red eyes and a huge grin on her face.

"Oh dear," said the witch as she stood up. "Are you having fun?" she asked Sue.

"No not really," replied Sue, "it's a bit too noisy. I would rather be outside in the sunshine."

The witch pushed the end of her long nose with her finger. There was a cloud of pink smoke, and a flash, and Sue was gone.

Ben was watching the witch as Sue disappeared. He was just about to shout at the witch, when the witch disappeared as well. He just stood where he was, with his mouth open, and pointing to were Sue had been.

"She's gone; she's gone!" he shouted to the others, who had not seen the disappearance of Sue.

"Where has that stupid witch sent Sue now?" he shouted. "The stupid witch has disappeared as well, so I don't know how to find out where she has gone, please help," he continued, shouting.

The remaining group of animals gathered around Ben, who was jumping up and down and stamping a foot on the ground with anger.

"Did you recognise the witch who made Sue disappear?" Mr Mole asked.

"Yes, it was Witch Clumsy," replied Ben, looking all around, and peering into the darkness.

"Let's try to get help from a different witch", Mrs Mole said, with concern in her voice. "Witch Clumsy is so clumsy, she might make things worse if we ask her again."

"Let's stay together," said Mr Wood the mouse, as he crept forwards from behind Mr Red the squirrel, where he had been hiding.

The group moved forward towards the busy crowd. A jolly elf asked if they needed any help, but before anyone could answer he ran away laughing, and started playing with another elf.

A group of fairies fluttered and danced in front of Mr Red the squirrel, who was leading the way around the cave.

As they entered the array of witches, elves, fairies and gnomes, the noise became louder, as everyone seemed to be very excited. Then, all of a sudden, the noise stopped, as if a switch had been turned off. All of the witches were looking in one direction, towards the inside of the cave. The fairies, elves and gnomes stood very silent and still, as they all looked in the same direction. Not a word was spoken, no a noise was made; nobody moved.

The animals, and Ben, also stood very still, and looked at one another.

A very bright light appeared, deep into the cave, with a small black shadow in front of the light.

The shadow moved forward and disappeared behind a very high desk on very high legs, with a chair to match, behind the desk. The light moved forward following the small black shadow until it lit the desk and the chair. All that could be seen was the small face of a tiny man, wearing a black top hat and a green coat.

The tiny man put his thumb in his mouth, and blew, and blew, on his thumb. Each time he blew on his thumb, he became bigger and bigger, until he was the right size to be behind the desk, and sitting in the chair.

Everybody and everything were still and very silent, watching the man very closely.

Mr Mole, leaned towards Ben's ear, and whispered very quietly, "It's Walt the Wizard."

Chapter 7
The Wizard

All the witches pushed forward through the crowd of fairies, elves and gnomes to stand in front of Walt the Wizard. By now the light was shining on Walt the Wizard, like a very strong spotlight. He had a very happy, friendly face as he looked at the group of witches in front of him. He raised both hands to the rim of this top hat. He tried to remove the hat, but it would not move he tried again, but the hat stayed firmly on his head.

"Thank you all for coming to this meeting," said the wizard looking at the witches, and recognising each one.

The elves, fairies and gnomes were now peering at the wizard from any high vantage point they could find. One gnome was standing on top of a stalagmite, his big hat was protecting him from the drips of water, dripping from the stalactite above.

Some fairies were fluttering, silently in the air above the witches. All were watching Walt the Wizard, in silence.

The wizard continued, "As you all know, some of you have new spells. As it is our custom, all new spells have to be shared with one another and approved by myself, before use. I know that some spells are used without my approval, that is when they go wrong."

There was a mumble of agreement amongst the audience. Witch Clumsy leaned across, and whispered something into another witch's ear.

"I think the Wet Witch has a new spell. Please tell us all," continued Walt the Wizard,

The Wet Witch moved forward to the front of the crowd, leaving puddles of water behind her. She stood in front of the wizard, and said, “I have invented a spell so that, whenever it rains, your shoes change into long rubber boots, to keep your feet dry. I have called them Wellingtons.”

There was a grown from the audience, and the wizard said, “That has already been invented. Spell not accepted; next please.”

“I have another spell,” said the Wet Witch, with excitement, “I have a canopy that protects your head whenever it rains, I have called it an umbrella.”

There was an even louder groan from the rest of the witches.

“That also has already been invented. Spell denied,” the wizard said, looking very unhappily at the witch.

The witch turned around and returned to her place. A hand rose from the middle of the witches. The hand rose further, and further, into the air on a very long arm. The hand started to wave on the end of the long arm.

“Yes, Witch Big Feet? I think you have a new spell for us to consider. I can see your long arm waving at me,” the wizard addressed the witch.

“I have invented a spell,” said the witch. “When you want to find a bug, but cannot see it, my spell makes the bug hum, so you can hear where it is. I call it *Humbug*. I have another spell that makes bugs disappear.”

“Well done,” said Walt the Wizard, scratching his forehead under the rim of his hat. “If your spell makes bugs go away, why do you need your *Humbug* spell? I will accept the *Disappearing Bug* spell, but not the *Humbug* spell."

The wizard, was about to ask for another witch to present a spell when he saw a flash of light from the audience. The flash of light was a reflection from Mr Mole's spectacles. The wizard stood up. He put his thumb into his mouth and blew very hard. As he blew, he grew in size until he could see right over the crowd in front of him.

He leaned over the crowd, and said, "Arthur Mole, what are you doing here?"

Everybody turned to look at Mr Mole. There was a rushing sound, as everyone took in a very deep breath in amazement at what they saw, as this was a very private meeting.

All the animals and Ben looked around the audience with wide eyes, thinking that perhaps they should not be at the meeting.

The wizard started to walk towards the small group, but hit his hat on the ceiling as he was so big. He stopped, put his thumb into his mouth, and sucked hard on the thumb. As he did so he shrank and shrank, until he was the same size as Mr Mole. The wizard was then able to walk towards Mr Mole and his friends.

Mr and Mrs Mole knew Walt the wizard, and how kind a wizard he was, so they were not worried about speaking with him; but in front of all these witches, well that was different.

Walt the wizard was now standing in front of Mr Mole and his friends.

"You have obviously come here for an important reason, because I can see you have brought your wife and friends?" The wizard asked.

Mr Mole replied. "We were brought here by Witch Forgetful. She thought somebody could help us with our problem."

The wizard turned to the rest of the audience, and said, "I have an important meeting with this group. Please enjoy yourselves for the moment. I will return soon, to continue with the new spells meeting."

The wizard turned to talk again to Mr Mole, but the noise returned, very loudly from the witches, fairies, gnomes and elves, as they all started talking about the visitors and the interruption to the meeting. Mr Mole could not hear what the Wizard was saying because of the noise.

The wizard made hand signals to follow him, so, all the animals and Ben followed the wizard through a very thick, wooden door into another room.

The wizard closed the door, and the noise disappeared behind it.

The room had a fire burning in a lovely fireplace, and surrounded by very comfortable-looking chairs. The Wizard stood with his back to the fire, with his hands behind his back. He invited the others to sit in the comfortable chairs.

"Please tell me about the problem," asked the wizard.

Mr Mole told the whole story, about the farmer wanting to dig up the hedge bank, the possible loss of their home in the bank, how they arrived in the cave, and all of their adventures on their journey so that they could tell Walt the Wizard. He also told of the disappearance of Sue, who they are all very worried about, and that they must find her.

Walt the Wizard thought for a moment before he said, "Please do not worry about Sue, she is very safe. When you next see her, she will give you some interesting information."

The wizard clapped his hands together, very loudly. He then put his hands deep in his trouser pockets.

"The spell has now been set, and I now feel very content that all will be well," said the wizard.

"Did he say we will have to live in a tent?" Walter Vole said to Mr Wood the mouse.

"No, he said he was content, not a tent," replied Mr Wood the mouse.

The wizard opened his arms wide, as if to welcome someone. As he did so, there was a flash of blue smoke, and there, stood in the middle of the smoke, was Sue.

All of the others were very relieved to see Sue again. They all started to ask her questions at the same time.

Before Sue could answer, the wizard said, "You must now return to your part of the wood, and tell everyone about the spell that I have set. As a result of my spell all will be well. When you get there, the children must drink two drops of dew from a snowdrop, to return them to their normal size. Good luck."

The wizard clapped his hands very loudly. Instantly the animals and children were outside Mr and Mrs Mole's front door, all of them sitting on the floor.

They all picked themselves up and brushed themselves down.

"Where have you been, what have you seen? What did you hear, what is this news?" Ben asked Sue, very excitedly.

"When I left all of you, I found myself in our kitchen, at home. Our father was talking to the farm manager about the fields. Father told the farm manager that he was not going to grow crops any more, but he will be putting sheep in the fields, so Father will be keeping the hedge banks, and hedges to keep the sheep safely in the fields."

When the animals heard this, they all started jumping about, clapping their paws together, and shrieking with joy.

Mr Mole stepped forward with two snowdrops in his hand.

"Thank you very much for helping us to save our homes. We have enjoyed being with you. Now we know how to make you small and large again, you are welcome at any time."

He handed the snowdrops to the children, who each drank two drops of dew from inside the flowers.

Ben and Sue felt very funny. Everything went very fuzzy. They found themselves leaning against the hedge bank. Everything seemed to be the right size again. No matter how hard they tried, they could not see the little door that led into Mr and Mrs Moles house.

Feeling very confused, Ben and Sue ran home to the farm. As they entered the farmyard, Ruffles their dog was waiting for them, wagging his tail. There was a very large lorry, and lots of men unloading sheep from the lorry.

Sue and Ben looked at each other, and smiled. Was it a dream, or did it really happen?

Mike Gauld.